Nicholas —
Keep reading!
your friend,
[signature]
2014

THE BARKING MOUSE

Antonio Sacre

illustrated by Alfredo Aguirre

Albert Whitman & Company
Morton Grove, Illinois

Glossary of Spanish Words
(not translated in story text)

adiós	goodbye
familia	family
flaco	skinny, thin
fútbol	soccer
gato	cat
hermana	sister
hermano	brother
hola	hello
ratón	mouse
¡Yo soy Papá Ratón!	I am Papa Mouse!
Yo voy a darle	I'm going to give him

In Cuba, medianoches are hot ham and cheese sandwiches on sweet bread—their name means "midnight" because they are often eaten as a late-night snack! Pollo frito is fried chicken. Congrí is a dish of rice and black beans.

Library of Congress Cataloging-in-Publication Data
Sacre, Antonio, 1968-
The barking mouse / by Antonio Sacre; illustrated by Alfredo Aguirre.
p. cm.
Summary: A Spanish-speaking mouse family enjoys their picnic until a cat threatens them, and the mother mouse must save the day by demonstrating her ability to speak another language. Story is interspersed with various Spanish words.
ISBN 10: 0-8075-0571-4
ISBN 13: 978-0-8075-0571-7
[1. Mice–Fiction. 2. Cats–Fiction.] I. Aguirre, Alfredo, ill.
I. Title. PZ7.S1226 Bar 2003[E]–dc21 2002012881
Text copyright © 2003 by Antonio Sacre.
Illustrations copyright © 2003 by Alfredo Aguirre.
Published in 2003 by Albert Whitman & Company,
6340 Oakton Street, Morton Grove, Illinois 60053-2723.

The artwork for this book was rendered in acrylics on Fabriano paper.
The typeface is Cafeteria.
The design is by Mary-Ann Lupa.

For more information about Albert Whitman & Company, please visit our web site at www.albertwhitman.com.

For Mimi, who told me this story. I wish I could tell it back to her now. A.S.

A mis padres que sin ellos nada soy. (To my parents—I am nothing without them.) A.A.

When my father came over to America from Cuba, he didn't speak a word of English. He only spoke Spanish. He met a woman who didn't speak a word of Spanish. She only spoke English. Do you know what happened? They got married, and they had me. I grew up speaking Español with my papá and English with my mom.

I was born on September 23, 1968, and on September 23, 1969, my mother gave birth to twin boys. That was my very first birthday gift! We were a handful for my parents, but luckily for us, our grandmother Mimi moved in. She only spoke Spanish, and the first thing she did when she came to our house in Delaware was give us all nicknames. She called me "Papito," a name typically given to first-born Cuban males. It loosely translates as "little boy" or "little man." When my brothers and I grew out of diapers, Mimi moved back to Miami.

In kindergarten, kids made fun of my nickname, calling me "Dorito," "Nacho Cheese Head," "Burrito," and even "Potato." They also made fun of my speaking Spanish, and so like many children of immigrants, I changed my name so it would sound more American. I went by "Tony" and I refused to speak Spanish ever again. If my father tried to talk to me in Spanish, I would answer back in English, or else pretend I didn't understand him. Eventually he spoke to me only in English. I began to forget my other language, and by the time I was a teenager, I could only understand and say very few words in Spanish.

I went to visit Mimi when I was in high school. When she saw that I could barely speak Spanish, she got so mad she threw food at me until I learned it again. She also told me stories. In her living room after her magical meals, I heard her Cuban friends tell many versions of my favorite story, the barking mouse. Sometimes it featured a Cuban mouse and an American mouse running into an American cat; other times a mouse from Havana and a *guajiro* (country) mouse encountered a city cat. I've read a version of the story from Uruguay, where two cats bark like dogs to trick the mouse into thinking the coast is clear—and when the mouse peeks out of his hole, they have a tasty little snack. Mean old cats!

The details vary, but the basic story is the same: it shows how language is a key to surviving the difficulties of a new place, and it also shows the value and joy of being bilingual. Thank goodness for Mimi!

Antonio Sacre

Once upon a time there was a family of mice. There was Mamá Ratón, Papá Ratón, and Brother and Sister Ratón. They all went on a picnic on a beautiful day.

Mamá had a beautiful voice and sang as she walked.

Papá had big muscles (or so *he* thought). He carried a *huge* picnic basket.

Sister was older than Brother and was very brave. Brother had big muscles like his dad (or so *he* thought) and was almost as brave as his sister. "Boo!" said Sister. "Yikes!" said Brother.

As they searched for a place to eat, they passed a tall fence.

"Psst! Hermana! I hear a cat lives behind this fence!" said Brother.

"I'm not scared of any cat," said Sister.

"Me, neither," said Brother.

Mamá sang a pretty song while Brother and Sister helped Papá unload the food.

Papá said, "Here are the medianoches, and the pollo frito, and the congrí, and the bread, and the lemonade. What are *you* all going to eat?"

"Papá, you are so bad!" said Mamá.

"I have to eat a lot to keep these muscles so huge!" said Papá.

When they were done eating, Brother and Sister said, "Mamá, Papá! Vamos a jugar. We want to go play."

"Children, you go play by yourselves," said Mamá. "Me and Papá, we're going to stay here and smooch."

Papá said, "Yippee!" And they started smooching. *Smmooocch!*

Brother and Sister said, "Eeewwww!" So they went to play by themselves.

They played hide-and-go-seek.
Sister was *always* It.

They played fútbol. Sister scored again!

They played "close your eyes
and spin till you fall down."
They *both* won!
They had a great time.

They went to check on Mamá and Papá.
Mamá and Papá were still smooching.
Smmooocch!
"Eeewwww!"
So Brother and Sister
went and played some more.

Sister said, "Race you to that fence, Hermano!"
Brother said, "That's where that cat lives!"
Sister said, "Chicken!"
Brother said, "I'm no chicken. Look at these muscles!"
"Boo!" said Sister. "Yikes!" said Brother. Then they
raced to the fence! Sister touched it first. But Brother
was not too far behind.
Brother said, "Do you think the cat is there?"
Sister said, "Let's look." They both looked through
the fence. Sure enough, there was the cat!

Sister said, "¡Hola, Gato!"

Brother said, "¡Hola, Gato!" The cat didn't say a word.

Brother said, "¡Hola, Gato!"

Sister said, "¡Hola, Gato!" The cat didn't move a whisker.

Brother flexed his muscles and said, "¡Hola, Gato flaco! You're no match for these! Hee hee hee!"

Sister said, "¡Hola, Gato flaco! Hee hee hee!" They both laughed so hard they had to hold their sides.

They laughed so hard that they didn't see the cat's bright green eyes get a little smaller.

They looked through the fence again. The cat stared back.

Sister stuck out her tongue and gave the cat a great big raspberry.

"Pplllllllllhhhhhhhhhhhhhh!"

So did Brother. "Pplllllllllhhhhhhhhhhhhhhh!"

They fell over laughing, tears coming out of their eyes.

They laughed so hard they didn't see the cat's tail stop
moving. They laughed so hard that they didn't see his claws
digging into the earth. They were laughing so hard . . .

they didn't see that cat jump up to the top of that fence and look down at them.

Brother and Sister stopped laughing. They looked up.
"Uhhh! ¡Adiós, Gato!" they said.

Then they turned around and started running as fast as they could.

"Mamá! Papá!" yelled Brother.
WHOOSH! They could hear the cat
running behind them! WHOOSH!
It was getting closer–
WHOOSH–and closer.

"Mamá! Papá!" yelled Sister.
WHOOSH! The cat was getting even
closer–WHOOSH–and closer!

Finally, they reached the picnic blanket. *Smmooocch!*

"Mamá, Papá! Stop smooching!" they shouted.

Papá turned around. "What?" he said.

"¡Papá, el gato!" said Brother.

"The cat is gonna eat us!" said Sister.

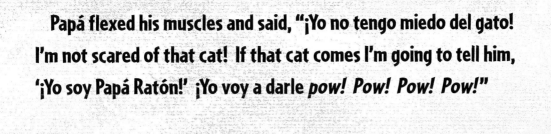

Papá flexed his muscles and said, "¡Yo no tengo miedo del gato!
I'm not scared of that cat! If that cat comes I'm going to tell him,
'¡Yo soy Papá Ratón!' ¡Yo voy a darle *pow! Pow! Pow! Pow!*"

And just then Papá saw the cat.
"Mamá!" he shouted. He jumped behind Mamá.
Then Brother and Sister jumped behind Mamá!

The only thing that stood between that mean cat
and her familia was Mamá. Her heart pounded.

She didn't know what to do, but with the courage a mother feels when her family is threatened, she stood on her hind paws, looked right into the great green eyes of that cat, and, from somewhere deep inside her, she said . . .

The cat stopped and thought, *This is weird. A barking mouse!*
No vale la pena. *It's not worth it,* the cat decided. He turned
around, jumped over the fence, and was gone.

"Whoa," said Brother.

"Cool!" said Sister.

"I knew I married the right woman!" said Papá.

And when they all got home nice and safe, Mamá said,
"You see, kids? ¡Es muy importante hablar otro idioma!
It pays to speak another language!"